CHRISTMAS JOKES FOR KIDS

1. What do you call an elf who releases an album?

a.A wrapper.

2.Why would Jay Z make a good elf?

a.   Because he's good at wrapping.

3.Why are there only 25 letters in the alphabet at Christmastime?

a.   Because there is noel.

4.What do you call someone who is scared of Santa?

a.Claustrophobic.

5. Which of Christopher Columbus's ships is Kris Kringle's favorite?

a. The SANTA Maria.

6. Which of Santa's reindeer is the most obnoxious?

a. RUDEolph.

7.Why are Santa's little helpers so insecure?

*a. Because
they have low elf esteem.*

8.What is the biggest kind of elf?

a.An elfephant.

9.What do you call it when Santa's little helper takes a photo of herself?

a.An elfie.

10.What do you get when you cross Jack Frost and Dracula?

a.Frost bite.

11.What is the best Christmas carol to sing on your porch?

a.   *Deck the Halls.*

12.Why did Santa get his sleigh for free?

a.Because it was on the house.

13.Who brings you presents when you're at the beach?

a.Sandy Claus.

14.Who brings presents to cats?

a.Santa Claws.

15.Who brings presents to dogs?

a.Santa Paws.

16.Who steals from the rich, gives to the poor, and wraps presents?

a.Ribbon Hood.

17.What do you get when you cross a Christmas tree and an iPhone?

a.A pineapple.

18.What day comes before Christmas Eve?

a.Christmas Adam.

19.What do you say to make Santa stop moving?

a."Santa, pause."

20.What does Kris Kringle wear?

a.Santa Clothes.

21.Where does a snowman make a deposit?

a.At the snowbank

22.What does Frosty do when he races in his car?

a.   *He snowdrifts.*

23.What do you call it when Frosty starts getting tired?

a.Snow drifting to sleep.

24.What do you get when you cross a musician and a book?

a.Rapping paper.

25.What do you call a snowman in July?

a.A puddle.

26.What does Santa use to walk when he gets hurt?

a.   A candy cane.

27.Where does Santa stay when he's out of town?

a.In a ho ho hotel.

28.What does Santa feel when he's out of town for a while?

a.Ho ho homesick.

29.What do you say to a snowman when he's acting rambunctious?

a.　　　　　"Chill out."

30.Why should you never send a Christmas gift to the future?

a. Because then it wouldn't be present.

31.What do you call it when Santa gives a speech?

a.A PRESENTation.

32.What did the snowman say to the other snowman?

a.Smells like carrots.

33.What do you say when you have a wedding on Christmas?

a."Marry Christmas."

34.How do you say "Merry Christmas" to a sheep in Spanish?

a."Fleece Navidad."

35.What kind of motorcycle does Santa ride?

a.A Holly Davidson.

36.What do you call it when you send a letter to Santa up the chimney?

a.Blackmail.

37.Why does Santa get sick every Christmas?

a.Because he comes down (with the) flu.

38.Why does Santa carry an umbrella with him?

a.Because of the raindeer.

39.What does Rudolph call his wife?

a.Reindear.

40.Where does Santa hang his suit?

a.In the clauset.

41.What do you call Santa's workshop on the weekend?

a.Claused.

42.What do Santa's kids do when they get home from school?

a. Their ho ho homework.

43. What do you hang on Christmas when you're in the army?

a.   *Missile-toe.*

44. What does Santa use to trim his nails?

a.   *Mistletoe-nail clippers.*

45.Why did Santa not have a job anymore?

a.Because he got sacked

46.What do you say when Santa's working the runway?

a."Sleigh!"

47.What is always falling and falling but doesn't get hurt?

a.Snowflakes.

48.What do you call Frosty when he cancels plans?

a.Snowflakey.

49.What do Santa's little helpers learn in kindergarten.

a.The elfabet.

50.What does Santa use in the garden?

a.The hoe, hoe, hoe.

51.What do you say to Santa when he hasn't shaved?

a.Hairy Christmas.

52.How do Santa's elves get their kids to soccer practice?

a.In their minivan.

53.What is an Elf's favorite dessert?

a.Strawberry short cake.

54.What kind of cereal did the snowman eat for breakfast?

a.   Snowflakes.

55.What is a snowman's favorite menu item from Wendy's?

a.A frosty.

56.What kind of car did Santa's elf buy?

a.A Toy-ota.

57.Why did Santa take his Christmas tree to the barbershop?

a.To get it trimmed.

58.What do you call an angel pointing 90 degrees?

a.A right angel.

59.What do you call Santa when he goes bankrupt?

a.Saint Nickel-less.

60.What do you call Santa when he's run out of sandwich toppings?

a.Saint Pickel-less.

61.What was the librarian's favorite Christmas carol?

a.Silent Night.

62.Why did Frosty the Snowman wear sunglasses?

a.Because he was so cool.

63.What did the snowman say to the other when they were moving a heavy couch?

a.Freezy does it.

64.Why was Frosty the Snowman sneezing?

a.Because he caught a cold.

65.Who is Santa Claus's favorite Rock-n-roll singer?

a.Elfis Presley.

66.What is a rabbit's favorite part of a snowman?

a.His nose.

67.What do baseball player snowmen wear on their heads?

a.Snowcaps.

68.Where does a queen put her husband's Christmas gifts?

a.In his stocKING.

69.Why is Santa a good presidential candidate?

a.Because he's always up in the poles.

70.What do you get it when you cross a fish, a heater, and a snowman?

a.A tuna melt.

71.What kind of money does Santa use?

a.Jingle bills.

72.Which elf comes after the eleventh?

a.The twelf.

73.What do you call a six-month-old snowman?

a.Water.

74.What did Frosty the Snowman's friend sing at his birthday?

a.   *"Freeze a Jolly Good Fellow."*

75.Why is it always so cold on Christmas?

a.Because it's in Decemberrrrr.

76.How did Frosty the Snowman lose weight?

a.   He waited for it to get warmer.

77.What Christmas carol do you sing in the Amazon rain forest?

a."Jungle Bells."

78.Who brings presents to sharks at Christmas?

a.Santa Jaws.

79.What do you call Santa when he goes down the chimney while the fire is still lit?

a.Crisp Kringle.

80.How are bad knitters like dead Christmas trees?

a.They both drop needles.

81.What bad toy will always win in a race?

a.A broken drum – you can't beat it.

82.Why did Santa's helper keep all the candy for himself?

a.Because he was sELFish.

83.What is Santa's little helper's favorite kind of seafood?

a.ShELFish.

84.Where does Santa store his books?

a.On the shELF.

85. How does Kris Kringle solve crimes?

a. *He follows the Santa Clues.*

86. How will you feel during Christmas time?

a. Yule be happy.

87. What is it called when a donkey and a horse celebrate Christmas?

a.Muletide.

88. What do you call it when the ocean rises on Christmas?

a. Yule-tide.

89.What is a reindeer's favorite Olympic sport?

a.The North Pole-vault.

90.Why are Santa and penguins so different?

a.   Because they are polar-opposites.

91.What do you call Santa with mood swings?

a.Bi-polar.

92.What do you call it when all the elves clap?

a.   Santapplause.

93. What do you call Santa's legal document?

a. A Santa Clause.

94. What did the wolf say to the other wolf on Christmas?

a. Happy howlidays.

95. What did the male sheep say to the female sheep on Christmas?

a. "Merry Christmas to ewe."

96. What do you say when Christmas dinner is burnt?

a. "Merry Crispness."

97. What comes at the end of Christmas?

a. The letter "s."

98. Where did the elf go to become a movie star?

a. To HOLLYwood.

99. What do you get when you cross sugar and an old man's walking stick?

a. A candy cane.

100. What's black and white and red all over?

a. A candy cane that got dropped in the fireplace.

38907486R00030

Made in the USA
Columbia, SC
08 December 2018